For Harriet, with much love

Read the whole series:

FRIDAY

This is me, Dorothy Constance Mae Louise, but all of my friends just call me ⚡Dot!⚡

And here is my family: Mum, my twin brother and sister, Alf and Maisy, and my dog, McClusky.

Rushing to school in an absolute **BLUR** today, *extremely* excited, because it's the last day of term and then **THE SUMMER HOLIDAYS BEGIN!**

In class our teacher, Mr Dickens, says, "Today we will play *games* instead of having lessons!"

We all whoop and shout, "Yay! Hooray! Wowzers!" until Frankie gets carried away with *his* "Wowzers!" and sends a pile of books flying.

We play board games and bingo. Amy crosses her numbers off first and wins a pair of **googly-eye glasses!**

And then we play **Who Am I?**

We get into pairs and each person
has a name they can't see written on a
post-it note stuck to their forehead.

You ask your partner questions
about who you are, but they can only
answer **"YES"** or **"NO"**.

Me and my best friend Beans are
in a pair and we are REALLY
QUICK to guess who we are!

This is because we are not *just* best
friends, OH NO . . .

We are also TOP
super-sleuthing
secret agents,
the Join the Dots
Detectives!

JOIN
THE DOTS
DETECTIVES

Which makes us very good at asking
the right questions and super-speedy
at finding out the **vital facts**.

Heading to the school gate at going-home time, everyone is talking about what they will be doing on their holidays.

The EXTRA-FANTASTIC

thing about this summer is that me (and the twins and Mum and McClusky) and Beans (and his dad) are going on holiday to the same place TOMORROW!

We are going to

Sunny Glades Campsite

by the seaside.

I CAN'T WAIT!!

15

"Are you bringing your detective kit, Beans?" I ask.

"I'm bringing a FEW things, like my torches and my code book," says Beans. "You just never know . . ."

eye patch

I have my packing list in my pocket. I add some essential stationery for drawing maps, making suspect lists and writing down clues, just in case.

sun hat

bathing costume

snorkle

lobster beach robe

flip-flops

notebook

TOP SECRET

pens

We walk home via the high street for some last-minute holiday shopping.

Mum buys sun cream that –

MMMMMmm! – smells like BUBBLEGUM...

The twins choose some tiny paper flags for their **sandcastles** . . .

and I choose some holiday *stickers*.

At home, me and McClusky try on LOTS of *different* sunglasses. We absolutely *cannot* decide which suit us best, so we pack them all.

SQUEEEEEEEZE! There's JUST room in my suitcase for my **extra-big** new puzzle book I've been saving specially ...

BUMPER HOLIDAY PUZZLE BOOK 1000's of hours of FUN !!!

and we are all packed and ready for the morning!

Saturday

We get up really early. The caravan is
hitched up . . .

The car is PACKED FULL
TO BURSTING ...

and we're off!

McClusky goes **crazy** with joy on car journeys. I give him a Calming Chew Doggy Treat every now and again and he settles down, but still **wriggles** in his sleep as if he's already imagining **running** across the beach!

And here we are – arriving at
Sunny Glades Campsite!
We drive in and park our caravan.
On one side is a wood, and on the
other an **enormous** tent with lots
of little children rushing in and out.

Inside, our caravan is like a little
house – everything the same but
small! A little fridge, a little oven ...

The floor is **red**-and-white check, and there are strawberry-patterned curtains *all* the way round, with cushions to match.

We unpack our things. The seats fold
out into beds and we arrange our
sleeping bags in a row.

Then I hurry over to find Beans.
His dad is **struggling** to get their
tent up, so
Mum sorts
it out while
he puts the
kettle on their
camping stove
and searches
for teabags and
biscuits.

It's *even smaller* inside their tent, with room for just two airbeds. Me and Beans take it in turns to **blow** them up with the **foot pump**. It's HARD WORK!

"The simple life for us, back to nature!" says Beans's dad, nibbling a digestive, while Mum hammers in a tent peg.

When we have finished unpacking, me, Beans and the twins explore the campsite. We see **crazy golf** and a **brilliant** playground ... "And look, Beans!" I say. **"Bicycles for hire!** I would LOVE to do some cycling."

There's a big farmhouse where the campsite owners live, and a campsite café called the Nook. It's a caravan too, but a tiny one with a stripy sunshade and **sparkly** bunting. There are little tables arranged round it, with a vase of *fresh flowers* on each one.

A teenager waves at us through the hatch. She looks **SO COOL**. I have never seen anybody with *turquoise* hair before! The twins can't stop staring.

"Hi, guys!" she says to us with a **huge** smile. "I'm Poppy. Welcome to the Nook! Come and have a look around."

The Nook may be small, but it has a

LOT

of **interesting** things.

32

Bric-a-brac is laid out for sale on a table beside the caravan – all kinds of *ornaments* and cups and saucers that don't match. Beans is fascinated by the **fossil collection**.

Mum has given me some money
to buy us all a **treat** for tea. "What
would you like?" I ask the twins. Alf
chooses a pink cupcake and Maisy

chooses a *yellow* one. After much

discussion, me and Beans go for the
warm mini doughnuts.

"I *love* doughnuts!" I tell Poppy. "And

so does my dog, McClusky!" I put a
little piece in my pocket to give to
him later.

"Doughnuts are *my life*," says Poppy. "I want to be a chef one day – baking will be my *speciality!*"

Me and Beans agree that these are the **BEST** doughnuts we've ever tasted.

"*Good!*" says Poppy. "I hope you come and hang out at the Nook *lots!*"

Poppy explains that her mum and dad own the campsite and she is in charge of the café. We can tell she works **really hard** – serving guests, bringing teas and clearing tables.

"It's **CRAZY** here, especially in the summer. I'll soon need a holiday myself," she laughs.

"Busy Poppy!" says Alf.

"Busy bee!" says Maisy.

Poppy is bringing out tea for two ladies, served in a teapot shaped like a **lighthouse**. "This is my **lucky teapot!**" she tells them.

"How beautiful, and *so* unusual!"
says the lady in a pink sunhat.

"Ooh, *yes!*" says her friend with a
yellow headscarf. "I wish *we* owned
one just like it – we collect teapots,
you know!"

The Nook is packed with guests. There's a **grumpy**-looking man at the table next to ours. He orders loads of *different* things to eat, but I notice he only takes **one** bite of each.

Weird!

I wonder who he is?

After we finish our teatime **treats**,
we wave goodbye to Poppy and
explore a bit more.

Over in the animal enclosure, we
meet Fred, a local boy who helps
look after the animals. He shows
us two donkeys, adopted from a
rescue sanctuary, called *Please* and

Thankyou ...

and some chickens . . .

and a tortoise called **Speedy**.

"He's **quicker** than you'd think," says Fred, "and **impossible** to spot when he heads off into the undergrowth – so we tie a **BALLOON** round him. That way, we always know where he is!"

Back in the caravan, we find our pyjamas and toothbrushes, settle in and draw the curtains, making everything **cosy** for the evening.

Now I'm **snuggled** down in my sleeping bag at bedtime. McClusky is snoring away in his basket, wedged in between me and the twins. I can still see some **sugar sprinkled** on his nose from the piece of doughnut I saved for him.

I

LOVE

Sunny Glades!

This holiday is going to be

FANTASTIC!

SUNDAY

When I wake up, the twins are still asleep, so I get up quietly and find Mum outside having a cup of tea. It feels really nice to be **up and out** of doors very early.

chirp!

chirp!

All we can hear are the birds

singing

and the leaves in the

trees.

Now McClusky **wakes up**, which means that soon everybody else for miles is **awake** too!

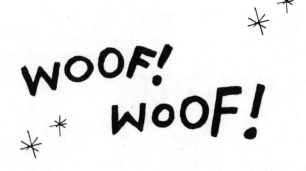

WOOF! WOOF!

The little children from the enormous tent next door are *running* around, *shouting* and shrieking.

An old couple in the caravan opposite peer **crossly** out of their open window. The woman is arranging some *flowers* on the windowsill. "So much for peace and quiet," the man grumbles, pulling the window shut.

We go over for breakfast at the Nook because Mum hasn't had time to go to the campsite shop yet for groceries.

The twins insist on wearing their big coats even though it's a warm, sunny day. They are whispering to each other in their secret *twinny* language too. They are **SO STRANGE** sometimes!

Beans and his dad are already here,
tucking into **cream-cheese bagels**.

We order our breakfast:
fresh croissants and

orange juice.

That grumpy man is here again,
standing a little way off and looking
over at the Nook.

"Who is that man?" we ask Poppy.

"Oh, that's Mr Blunt," she tells us.
"He has just opened a café himself,
right down by the sea, called
BLUNT'S BEACH CAFÉ."

A customer waves to Poppy and she rushes off again.

"Well, *we* won't be going to Blunt's," I whisper to Beans. The Nook is already our favourite café in the whole world!

Beans's dad wanders off with his binoculars to look at birds. Mum is concentrating on her shopping list while the twins finish their breakfast, so me and Beans go over to the playground to try out the tyre swing and the **wobbly** plank.

By the time we head back past the Nook, Mum and the twins have left.

We see Poppy on her hands and knees, looking under the tables.

OH NO – she looks very worried.

"My **lighthouse** teapot has VANISHED!" she says. "AND one of my vases of flowers! I can't see them *anywhere*! They are very special to me. Where can they be?"

What a calamity!
POOR POPPY!

I look at Beans and he looks at me.
**WE ARE BOTH THINKING
EXACTLY THE SAME THING.**

"There are two people who have
ALL the detectively skills to find the
missing teapot and vase—" I start to
say, and Beans finishes my sentence.

"US!!"

It's the **Sunny Glades** Mystery
and the Join the Dots Detectives are
ON THE CASE!!

Straight away we find a quiet place
for a secret Join the Dots meeting.

"Somebody must have **stolen** the teapot and vase of *flowers*!" I say.

"Yes!" says Beans. "But *who*?"

"We must make a list of suspects," I say.

We tour the campsite, keeping our eyes open for anyone acting **suspiciously.**

"What about those ladies who were having tea at the Nook yesterday?" I suggest. "There could be something fishy going on – **they actually COLLECT teapots!**"

We put them at the top of the list.

"And that cross old couple," says Beans. "Look – they have *flowers* on their windowsill. Maybe they wanted more!"

"And what about those little children from the **huge** tent?" I say. "I reckon they could be quite naughty!"

We see Fred go past, pushing a wheelbarrow **full** of straw. "And Fred!" says Beans. "Who knows what's under all that straw? We should add him too . . ."

I'm not really sure why Fred would want a teapot and a vase but I keep quiet. It's **important** to consider all possibilities.

lady in the pink sunhat
lady with the yellow headscarf
cross old couple
children from the huge tent
Fred

But there's no time to discuss it
further because Mum is calling me
over. She is making
a **picnic lunch**.
"Grab your things," she says. "We
are going to the beach!"

We meet up with Beans and his dad and follow the steep, stony path, winding down past **BLUNT'S BEACH CAFÉ**.

"Shall we add Mr Blunt to the
suspects list?" I ask Beans. "He was
at *the scene of the crime*."

"Yes, I think we should!" he says.

lady in the pink sunhat
lady with the yellow headscarf
cross old couple
children from the huge tent
Fred
Mr Blunt

We turn the corner and there is a little cove and **THE SEA**.

We do not waste one single second –
me and Beans *rush* straight into the
waves, and so does McClusky!

brrrr!

brrrrr!

EEK!!! It is MUCH **colder**
than I was expecting!

And it's MUCH harder to get out of a wet bathing costume than I expected too! Struggling to get changed inside a towel ... *Wriggling* and **wobbling** and *very* nearly falling over!

There is **sand** in the sandwiches but we don't care – the picnic is DELISH.

After lunch, we have a sandcastle
competition – Beans and Maisy
versus me and Alf.

The judges are my mum and Beans's
dad. They say that both sandcastles
are so *stupendously* good that we
are **ALL** winners.

We stay at the beach **all day**. When
we get back to the campsite, there's
just time to change into our warm,
snuggly clothes before heading over
to Beans and his dad's tent for our tea.

It's a **BBQ**, followed by s'mores: marshmallows toasted on the campfire, sandwiched between two biscuits with a layer of chocolate.

They taste INCREDIBLE.

While the grown-ups are chatting, Alf and Maisy are still whispering to each other and McClusky is busy licking the **BBQ** dishes, me and Beans discuss the case.

"We will use our list of suspects and investigate each one – first thing in the morning!" I say.

"Great plan, Dot!" says Beans.

"We need to ask some cunningly clever questions," I say, "like, 'Do you drink a lot of tea?' and, 'Aren't the *flowers* nice at this time of year?'"

"And how about, 'Do you like **lighthouses**?'" adds Beans.

Beans also shows me a new way for us to send vital secret messages to each other across the campsite: MORSE CODE! He takes two small torches out of his pocket and gives one of them to me.

"You can send a secret message across a long distance. Each letter is made up of a different combination of a short burst of light – **a dot** – **and a long one** – a dash!"

"Dot dash – that's me in a *hurry!*" I laugh.

Here is the whole alphabet.

```
A •—        J •———       S •••
B —•••      K —•—        T —
C —•—•      L •—••       U ••—
D —••       M ——         V •••—
E •         N —•         W •——
F ••—•      O ———        X —••—
G ——•       P •——•       Y —•——
H ••••      Q ——•—       Z ——••
I ••        R •—•
```

We try out our names ...

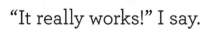

"It really works!" I say.

I use my new torch to look at the list of suspects again.

Hang on – what's this? Some of the note is missing!!!

Very strange . . .

lady in the pink sunhat
lady with the yellow headscarf
cross old couple
children from the huge tent
Fred
Mr Blunt

Monday

Straight after breakfast (Honey Nut
Crispies from the campsite shop –
YUM, my FAVE), Beans comes over.

He has drawn **a map** of the campsite.

"Fantastic map, Beans!" I say.

THE SEARCH BEGINS. Me, Beans and McClusky head over to the bicycle-hire shed.

"We will cover much more ground on bikes!" I say.

79

McClusky jumps up into my basket. He can be on lookout duty. He has a very good nose for sniffing out the **vital** clues.

First we cycle over to the camper van belonging to the ladies with the *pink* sunhat and the *yellow* headscarf. They are sitting at a picnic table reading their books.

Oh-so-casually, I say, "So, you collect teapots!"

"We *do!*" they say. "We've just bought these beauties at the local antiques market!" They proudly show us their rabbit teapot and their **cottage teapot** and another shaped like an aeroplane ...

but no, **no**

lighthouse teapot

here.

~~lady in the pink sunhat~~
~~lady with the yellow headscarf~~
cross old couple
children from the huge tent
Fred
Mr Blunt

Next we slow down near the
little children's huge tent to get a
good look at all the plates and mugs
washed up and laid out to dry . . .

but no lighthouse teapot and no
vase of *flowers*.

"Do you like lighthouses?" Beans asks
the children, but they just look at us,
puzzled.

Then we prop our bikes up against a tree near the **cross** old couple's caravan. Feeling very **nervous**, we **creep** round the side.

"You look first!" I whisper.

"No, YOU look first!" whispers Beans.

On tiptoe, we both pop up and **peep** inside.

Thank goodness there's no one there!
There ARE fresh *flowers* – but they
are in a different vase, not Poppy's.
No **lighthouse teapot** either.

~~lady in the pink sunhat~~

~~lady with the yellow headscarf~~

~~cross old couple~~

~~children from the huge tent~~

Fred

Mr Blunt

We find Fred chasing an escaped chicken round the enclosure.

"Hot work!" says Beans. "Is it your tea break soon?" (So clever and *cunning*!)

"No tea for me!" says Fred. "Can't stand the stuff!" And he gets a bottle of cola out of his overalls.

"It can't be Fred then," I say. "Why would he want a teapot? And I don't think he's a vase sort of person either."

"We only have one suspect left
on our list," says Beans. "Mr Blunt!"

~~lady in the pink sunhat~~
~~lady with the yellow headscarf~~
~~cross old couple~~
~~children from the huge tent~~
~~Fred~~
Mr Blunt

We return our bicycles and walk back.

At the Nook, we see Poppy balancing a **huge** pile of plates and teacups on one hand and putting up a notice for "Crafternoons" with the other.

Crafternoons!

Arty crafty fun at the Nook every Monday and Tuesday afternoon throughout the holidays

do come along!

I am so excited! Poppy's Crafternoons are activities for the families staying at the campsite. Today's activity will be *decorating* biscuits! **I REALLY** want to go and so do the twins.

Beans and his dad go out for the afternoon to see their Auntie Celia and Uncle Cecil who live nearby, so Mum takes McClusky for a walk and me and the twins go to the Crafternoon at the Nook.

"Why are you STILL wearing your big coats?" I ask the twins. "It's *so* hot today!" But they will **NOT** take them off. They are very *odd* sometimes!

Before we begin our *decorating*, Poppy brings out her special biscuits and gives each of us one to try.

"I've never tasted this flavour before," I say. "It's SO YUMMY!"

"Ah, yes," says Poppy. "These are my grandma's SECRET recipe! Here, let me show you..."

Poppy gets a book out of her apron pocket.

"It's my precious recipe book! This is where I keep all my very best recipes – I've been saving them for years... I reckon that you are just the right person to appreciate it!"

We turn the pages together, looking at all her notes and pictures. Poppy loves to **doodle** – just like me!

The twins are on ᵗⁱPtoe to see too,
but I am *so pleased* it was me Poppy
chose to show it to.

I LOVE

her recipe book –

it's amazing!

Poppy puts the recipe book down
on the counter, brings over more
biscuits and a selection of *toppings*
and we get started.

I am just concentrating on *decorating* my last biscuit while the twins **scamper** around and won't sit still.

Poppy is **clearing** away the

sugar sprinkles

and **blobs** of icing . . .

when she gives *a cry*.

The **sparkly** bunting has GONE!
Poppy feels inside her apron pocket …
looks at the empty counter …

HER RECIPE BOOK HAS GONE TOO!!!

OH NO! Another disaster

"What **IS** going on?" says Poppy. I see she is nearly in tears.

"Don't worry," I tell her, "I'm sure they will turn up." I don't know what else to say.

Just as we are leaving,
I see Mr Blunt again.

He is sneaking round the back of the
Nook and **peering** in through a small
window. Then he **stomps** away, back
down the path to his Beach Café.

HIGHLY

SUSPICIOUS.

Back at the caravan, McClusky is playing with a massive stick he's brought back from his walk. I lie on the rug, munching my biscuits, and do some crosswords in my extra-big new puzzle book, which always helps me

THINK.

First the **lighthouse teapot** and the vase
of *flowers*, now the **sparkly** bunting
and the recipe book . . .

And why is Mr Blunt hanging around the Nook, **peering** in through the window?

Is he involved in the disappearances?

I'm **itching** to discuss it with Beans, but he won't be back until after dinner with his aunt and uncle.

Now it's bedtime. This is my chance to get a message to Beans!

"I'm just having one last look at the lovely moon!" I say to Mum, and I step out into the **dark**. It feels exciting, being up and out of doors very late at night.

I get out my torch and send a morse code message across the campsite:

·· —· ···— · ··· — ·· ——· ·— — ·
—— ·—·
—··· ·—·· ··— —· —
— ——· —— ——— ·—· ·—· ——— ·—

**INVESTIGATE MR BLUNT
TOMORROW**

I only hope Beans is looking.

He is! Here comes his reply . . .

—.—— • •••

YES

Just getting into my sleeping bag, and – strange! I didn't notice it before, but some of the note with the morse code alphabet Beans gave me is **missing . . .**

Almost as if it has been N^IB_BL^ED!!

TUEsdAy

I don't even wait for breakfast – I grab an apple and *hurry* over to find Beans. But before we have even made a plan ...

"LOOK – it's Mr Blunt again!"** I say. The chance to investigate him came sooner than we expected!

This time we **follow** him at a distance, making sure he doesn't **spot** us.

He **sneaks** up on the Nook when Poppy isn't looking . . .

First he **snoops** around the tables, examining the leftovers and *muttering* to himself, "Hmmm, very interesting . . ."

Then he pins up a leaflet advertising **BLUNT'S BEACH CAFÉ** *right on top of*

the Nook's sign –

WHAT A CHEEK!

And now he is hiding behind a tree, taking photographs of the Nook's menu board!

That settles it – Mr Blunt is our number-one suspect!

"Mr Blunt MUST be the thief!" I say.

"But **WHY**?" says Beans.

"Is he jealous of the Nook?" I ask.
"Does he want to make *his* café look
prettier and *his* cakes taste better?"

"And that way he hopes to steal the
Nook's customers!" adds Beans.

"We **MUST** get down to the
beach today to check him out!" I say.

"We mustn't let him see us **snooping** around and guess we're on to him, though," says Beans. "He's seen us a lot at the Nook already."

I frown. "But how will we get close enough to

BLUNT'S BEACH CAFÉ without him seeing us?"

"I have a **brilliant** idea..." says Beans as his dad walks over.

"Dad," he says, "can you lend us your **binoculars**? We want to go bird-watching!"

"Sure!" says his dad.

I rush back to our caravan as fast as I can. "Please, please, *please* let's go to the beach RIGHT NOW!" I say to Mum. I am **SO IMPATIENT** to spy on Mr Blunt and to solve this case!

Mum looks at me, surprised. "OK!" she says. **"Hold your horses!"**

At the beach, we use the **binoculars** to spy on Mr Blunt from a distance.

We try and try, **peering** into the eyepiece and twiddling the focus, but it's still too **blurry** and **fuzzy** to see clearly into the café.

"Still **no** evidence!" I say. SO frustrating!

So we decide to leave it for now. We go snorkelling instead, then explore the rockpools with the twins. We see **a crab, a tiny fish** and lots of **limpets**.

We always take buckets
and **NEVER**
a net. These **sea**
creatures are really delicate –
getting tangled in a net can hurt them!

After we let the sea creatures
go, the twins fill their
buckets with pebbles.

These buckets are *heavy* – I WISH
I hadn't offered to carry them back
up the path!

After lunch we have **three** rounds of

crazy golf . . .

but I just

can't get

the ball

in through

the windmill door!

Today's Crafternoon activity is making a wind chime out of shells, bottle tops and teaspoons ...

Me and Beans go along, but we are too distracted discussing the case and our wind chimes end up a bit **wonky.**

ding!

ding!
ding!

In the evening, Beans's dad shows us how to make **monkey bread:** balls of biscuit dough rolled in *cinnamon sugar* and baked on the campfire.

"This is delicious!" says Mum. "You are such a **good cook!**"

While the grown-ups are exchanging recipes, me and Beans plan the next stage of solving the **Sunny Glades** Mystery.

"We must get a closer look at **BLUNT'S BEACH CAFÉ**," I say. "There's nothing else for it. We need to go **DEEP INTO ENEMY TERRITORY . . .**"

? ? ? ?

WEDNESDAY

Beans and his dad come over for breakfast – **sausage sandwiches** with fried onions and ketchup.

On any other day I would LOVE them, but today I am too **nervous** to eat more than a few bites.

Straight after breakfast, me and Beans persuade his dad to take us down to the beach.

On the way, we say hello to Poppy as she opens up the Nook. She is still *worrying* about the teapot and the vase and the bunting, but she misses her precious recipe book most of all.

"I just **can't** understand it!" she says.

"Don't worry – they will turn up **SOON!**" we say.

123

As Poppy brings out a tray of cakes and biscuits, this gives me an *idea.*

"We must try out lots of Mr Blunt's baking," I whisper to Beans, "to see if he has been using the recipes from Poppy's book!"

We don't bother with a swim or sandcastles or anything else... **Operation Enemy Territory** starts

NOW!

While Beans's dad is reading the newspaper, we walk right into Blunt's Beach Café. My heart is beating REALLY *fast* in my chest –

ba-do͞om-ba-do͞om-ba-do͞om . . .

We sit down at a table and look around. There is Mr Blunt, serving behind the counter. In his hand – a teapot! Above his head – bunting!! On the table – a vase of *flowers*!!!

Have we caught *him* **red-handed**?

No.

It's not the **lighthouse** teapot – just an ordinary one. It's not the Nook's bunting either – not **sparkly**, just drab and **plain**. When we look again, we see the *flowers* are **plastic**, not even real.

"We still need to try LOTS of cakes, though," whispers Beans. He is looking over at the cake stand and can't help licking his lips.

So we buy some biscuits and a cupcake, and then **another** cupcake and some mini doughnuts, and then Beans buys **one more** cupcake "just to be sure" …

But they are
not NEARLY
        as good as Poppy's.
The biscuits are just ordinary, nothing like Poppy's grandma's secret recipe.

Something catches my eye –
a poster on the wall advertising
**"Afternoon Activities
for all the Family"** . . .
It reminds me of Poppy's
Crafternoons – the same but NOT
the same.

Is Mr Blunt copying Poppy? Is that
why he has been *snooping* around
the Nook?

I have a

LIGHTBULB MOMENT.

"He's **stealing** the Nook's IDEAS!" I say.

"I think you're right! But we still have no proof," says Beans. "We must catch him in the act of **stealing ACTUAL THINGS!**"

This calls for

DRASTIC
action!

We make a SECRET plan ...

It's evening and starting to rain.
Time to put on our disguises and
catch the thief **red-handed**!

I have my
pineapple
sunglasses and my hooded
beach robe with a lobster
pattern on it.

Beans wears a baseball cap
and a
stripy windbreaker worn like a cloak.

We dodge the showers, **sneak** round the back of the Nook and hide behind a tree, peeping out. McClusky follows us – he always seems to know when he is needed. I'm glad he's here. He's not exactly fierce, but he is VERY protective.

Poppy has packed up all the **bric-a-brac** and is just about to close up for the day. While she is round the front, **stacking** the chairs, we **dash** into the tiny caravan and quickly hide in the broom cupboard.

Beans finds a lampshade and pops it on his head – now we look even more like the pile of old stuff you might find in a cupboard. McClusky hides behind a **bristly** broom that looks very like him. He is a MASTER OF DISGUISE.

"Be VERY quiet, McClusky!" I whisper. "It's really important!"

"Im-PAW-tant?" says Beans.

"Don't make me laugh!" I whisper urgently.

When I get the **giggles** in a super-tense situation, it can lead to

HYSTERICS.

We wait and wait, **peeping** out of a tiny high window, wondering what Mr Blunt might come to steal. Maybe Poppy's fossils, or her ornaments! Maybe her cups and saucers?

After a VERY

looooong

time...

a *huge, scary shadow* goes past.

We are *terrified* out of our **wits!!!**
The shadow looms closer and an eye
peers in at us.

I am so *frightened* I cannot even
scream.

IS IT MR BLUNT???

Massive

WHISKERY nostrils,

a rubbery pink tongue ...

NO – it is the donkey, *Please*. Or maybe it's Thankyou. It must have escaped from the enclosure, and is now wandering around the campsite – probably on the lookout for snacks.

I don't know whether I am more
disappointed or relieved, but when
we decide to call it a day and Beans
hurries back to his tent and me and
McClusky rush back to our caravan,

my legs feel like wobbly jelly.

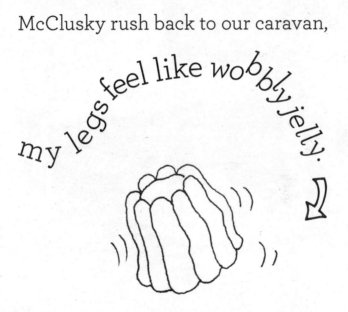

By now even the THOUGHT of
Mr Blunt scares me. I can hardly
bring myself to look at my **doodle**
of him, but when I do – half of it is
missing! What **IS** going on?
Is it sabotage??

Now there are TWO mysteries:

someone is stealing from the Nook, and something is happening to my **notes** and *doodles!*

Are these **two** mysteries connected?

It's night-time. I am woken up by the rain getting worse and worse, hammering on the roof, and the wind is **battering** against the windows.

There's a scritch-scratching noise *from under the caravan.*

scritch scratch

VERY creepy! I must be imagining it.

I put my head right inside my sleeping bag and try to get back to sleep.

Thursday

The rain has stopped, but because it rained so much in the night the grass has turned to **mud**. Alf and Maisy decide to roll down the **muddy** hill next to the play area.

They do it **again** and **again** and **again**...

The more **slippery** it gets, the *faster* they go and the better they like it. By now you can't even recognise them. They are two **mud-monsters** with feet.

And who joins in?
McClusky, of course!

Now the twins are making **mud** pies. *"Mmmm, yummy!"* they say. "It's our secret recipe!"

While Mum deals with McClusky and the **mud-monsters** in the shower, me and Beans have a hasty meeting of the Join the Dots Detectives.

Join the Dots Detectives HQ

We feel really down in the dumps. No evidence, no new clues. "What do we do now?" says Beans. But neither of us knows the answer.

Mum says, "You two look in the doldrums! Fancy an ice cream?"

After a cookies 'n' cream cone with a flake in it (me) and a strawberry choc-ice (Beans), we do feel a BIT better.

The twins turn down the chance of an ice cream, preferring to play in the wood.

strange!

Mum has given up trying to persuade them not to wear their big coats as they tramp to and fro.

We hang about at the campsite all morning, at a loose end. There's nothing worse than an unsolved case – but with **no new leads**, what can we do?

"Why not *play* with the twins?"

says Mum,

but they are busy emptying their

buckets and whispering in their ***twinny***

language, so they don't need us.

"How about some bird-watching up on the cliff?" Beans's dad asks us, but we're not that keen.

"Take McClusky for a nice long walk," says Mum, and we do.

Me, Beans and McClusky are just coming back past the Nook when we see Poppy at the hatch, looking very upset.

"A *fresh* batch of mini doughnuts –
VANISHED!!" she says.

The doughnuts!!!

That's the **_LAST STRAW._**
Poor Poppy.

The twins hurry over. "Come with us! Come with us!" they say.

But I'm hardly listening. "Not now," I tell them. This isn't the time for games – the case has taken an urgent new turn for the worse!

"Could it be one of the animals?" says Beans.

I think of the loose donkey yesterday and we rush to their enclosure. But there are *Please* and Thankyou, contentedly munching their hay . . .

We **run** over to the chicken coop,
but the gate is securely **locked . . .**

Then we spot Speedy the tortoise's
balloon in the undergrowth. Could he
be making off with a doughnut??

We chase the balloon to catch up with him. He is **surprisingly fast**!

Me in front, then Poppy, then Beans, then McClusky ... The twins follow, **running** along behind us ...

but no.
All Speedy
has in his
mouth is
a bit of
squashed
dandelion.

No sign of the mini doughnuts ANYWHERE.

The twins are *pulling* at our T-shirts. "Come with us!" says Alf.

"Not now," I say. "This *isn't* a good time!"

"PLEASE!" says Maisy.

And now I start to think . . .

Why have the twins been whispering *secretively* all week?

Why did they insist on wearing big coats in hot weather – could they have been hiding something underneath?

Why were they hanging around in the wood when they could have been having ice cream? And what were they emptying their buckets for?

"OK . . ." I tell them.

The twins lead us – me, Poppy, Beans and McClusky – to the wooded glade next to the caravan.

And here are the **lighthouse** teapot and the vase of *flowers*, and the **sparkly** bunting hanging up between the branches . . . and here are the **precious recipe book** and the mini doughnuts . . .

Alf and Maisy have made their own café in a little clearing amongst the trees!

IT WAS THE TWINS ALL ALONG!!!

For a few moments, I am exasperated and very cross. "It's **wrong** to take things that aren't yours . . ." I tell them.

But then I see their *happy*, proud faces, and how well they have improvised, with leaves for plates and cushions for seats. And then I see a handmade sign taped up on the trunk of a tree in their funny, childish writing:

Poppy's place

"You work so hard and you are SO BUSY!" Maisy says to Poppy.

"We wanted to make a special place just for YOU!" says Alf.

I am worried that Poppy will be angry ... but she just *laughs*!

"Thank you so much!" she says. "This looks *AMAZING!*"

And then she says, "Hang on a minute ..."

She hurries over to the Nook and
puts up her own sign:

CLOSED
back later!

"It's about time I took an
afternoon off!"

We all sit together in Poppy's Place.
We admire the **sparkly** bunting
and the *flowers* and Poppy shows
us some more of her special recipe
book ...

We **enjoy** the mini doughnuts –
McClusky especially – and they are
STILL the best we've ever tasted,
even though the sugar coating *might*
have got a bit mixed up with sand
from the twins' bucket ...

And we all have the
BEST TIME EVER,
relaxing in the sunshine.

Friday

The last day of the holidays!

But it's a lovely sunny day and there's
still time for one last ice cream and
one more round of **crazy golf**.

I knock the ball

right in **through**

the door of

the **windmill**.

YESSSSSSS!

And there's time for one last play on the beach. On the way down to the cove, we stop at a stream that goes alongside the path, right down to the sea. Perfect for a game of Poohsticks!

It's a race: we each choose a small stick, drop them into the water at the same time and see whose stick reaches the beach first.

We play again and again until everyone wins lots of races each.

So the **Sunny Glades** Mystery is solved.

It was the twins who took the missing things from the Nook, but they did it for a kind reason. Mr Blunt wasn't the thief after all, but he wasn't entirely innocent either. He *was* copying Poppy's ideas – that's why he was snooping around the Nook – and that is still a sort of stealing.

It didn't work, though – **BLUNT'S BEACH CAFÉ** isn't nearly as special as the Nook. It just goes to show you need to **think of your own ideas** if you want to be good at something!

But there's one last piece of **the puzzle**, though . . .

Who has been **nibbling** my notebooks??

"Oh, that must have been Walter," says Poppy, "the resident campsite mouse!"

Sure enough, when we hitch up and move the caravan, I see a little nest underneath made of **nibbled** pieces of paper from my notes!

So **THAT** was the scritch-scratching noise I heard on the night of the storm!

There's no sign of **Walter,** but when I look back at the picture of my *decorated biscuits* from the Crafternoon … there he is in the distance, hurrying off with a tiny scrap of paper. I hadn't spotted him!

We pack up the car and it is *even more* full of **stuff** – there's the twins' huge pebble collection, and McClusky insists on bringing his MASSIVE stick.

We say goodbye to Poppy.

"Come back SOON!" she says, giving us all a *big* hug.

There's just time for me to say to Beans, "That was our **trickiest** case of all – and the answer was right under our noses all along!"

"Yes!" says Beans. "See you back at home. There's lots of summer holiday left – **HOORAY!**"

goodbye! goodbye! goodbye!

Have you read?

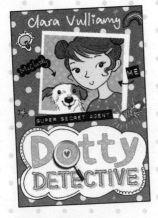

When someone seems set on sabotaging the school show, Dot is determined to find out how, and save the day!

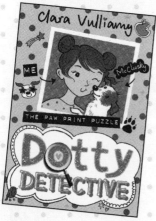

When Dot starts hearing strange noises at night, Beans is convinced there has to be something SPOOKY afoot. But, before they can be certain, Dot and Beans must GET PROOF.